Finding Luck

MARGUERITE HENRY'S Misty Inn

Finding Luck

By Kristin Earhart

Illustrated by Serena Geddes

ALADDIN
New York London Toronto Sydney New Delhi

This book is a work of fiction. Any references to historical events, real people, or real places are used fictitiously. Other names, characters, places, and events are products of the author's imagination, and any resemblance to actual events or places or persons, living or dead, is entirely coincidental.

ALADDIN

An imprint of Simon & Schuster Children's Publishing Division

1230 Avenue of the Americas, New York, New York 10020

First Aladdin paperback edition January 2016

Text copyright © 2016 by The Estate of Marguerite Henry

Illustrations copyright © 2016 by Serena Geddes

Also available in an Aladdin hardcover edition.

All rights reserved, including the right of reproduction in whole or in part in any form.

ALADDIN is a trademark of Simon & Schuster, Inc., and related logo is a registered trademark of Simon & Schuster, Inc.

For information about special discounts for bulk purchases, please contact Simon & Schuster Special Sales at 1-866-506-1949 or business@simonandschuster.com.

The Simon & Schuster Speakers Bureau can bring authors to your live event. For more information or to book an event contact the Simon & Schuster Speakers Bureau at 1-866-248-3049 or visit our website at www.simonspeakers.com.

Book designed by Laura Lyn DiSiena

The text of this book was set in Century Expanded.

Manufactured in the United States of America 1021 OFF

10 9 8

Library of Congress Control Number 2015957269

ISBN 978-1-4814-1423-4 (hc)

ISBN 978-1-4814-1422-7 (pbk)

ISBN 978-1-4814-1424-1 (eBook)

To Elinor, and everyone at Bridle Hill Farm

Finding Luck

Chapter 1

"STARBUCK, STOP THAT!" WILLA GIGGLED. THE pony snuffled Willa's shoulder and nibbled at the ends of her walnut-colored hair. Willa reached around and scratched the pony's whiskered chin.

"She's hungry," Ben said. He snapped stems of the clover that grew along the driveway, just out of the buckskin pony's reach. He held out the bouquet, tickling Starbuck's lips.

"How could she be hungry?" Mom asked, not even looking up from the garden patch she was weeding. "You give her fresh-picked treats all day."

Starbuck stretched out her neck and tried to lip at the white flower, but Ben quickly pulled it away.

"Please don't feed her any of the herbs and plants we're growing for the restaurant," Mom said, shaking a seed packet. Soon the kids' dad would be opening a restaurant right there, on the main floor of their house. It was going to be part of the family's bed-and-breakfast, which was called Misty Inn. Of course, they'd had only two guests so far, but they had all worked hard getting the old house ready.

"Don't tease her," Willa insisted. She scowled at her brother.

"I don't want to spoil her," Ben claimed. A sly smile played at the corner of his mouth.

"Just give it to her, Ben," Mom said, "but then call it quits. If you keep hand-feeding her, she'll forget how to graze like a normal horse."

Willa knew that wasn't true. Starbuck was too smart to forget something like that. Besides, grazing came naturally to horses.

"Sometimes I forget she's here," Ben confessed, combing his fingers through her black mane. "And it's like a big present when I look in the field."

"Me too," Willa agreed. "But sometimes it feels like she's always been here. Doesn't it?" It was a funny thing for Willa to say. After all, the Dunlaps hadn't lived at Misty Inn that long. It had been less than a year ago that their family had moved to Chincoteague Island. The large Victorian house was very different than their tiny apartment in the big city of Chicago.

Starbuck had come to live at Misty Inn several months later, in the fall. The pony had spent almost the whole summer at their grandma's rescue center. While she was there, the kids had helped Starbuck get better from a leg injury. After that, they had worried that Grandma Edna would find a new home for the sweet mare. Their grandma was very practical with the animals at the rescue center. "Miller Farm is not a place for pets," she often said.

In the end, it was clear that Starbuck was the one who chose her new home—and she chose to be with the Dunlaps. It was also clear that Grandma Edna understood that they belonged together.

Now it was spring. "It doesn't matter how long she's been here; it just matters that she stays here," Ben said.

Starbuck whinnied and threw her head in the air. "Starbuck agrees," Willa said.

Ben laughed, and their puppy, Amos, barked. With his tail wagging, he circled Ben's feet. Amos was new to Misty Inn too. He had arrived with Buttercup, a neighbor's horse who lived in the old barn.

The only one who had real history at the house was New Cat. As a stray, the tabby cat had enjoyed her afternoons on the sunny, warm porch.

In fact, that was where she was resting now. New Cat was sprawled out, her green eyes barely open. Her ear twitched at the sound of a motor. She forced her lazy eyes open as the noise came closer.

"It's Grandma!" Ben called, waving toward an old, red pickup truck that pulled into the driveway.

"Afternoon, Dunlaps," Grandma Edna said. She reached to pick up a package from the other seat. "I've got something for you."

"For me?" Ben asked. Willa shook her head.

"For all of you," Grandma said. The skin around her eyes crinkled when she smiled. "But mostly for your parents, I guess."

Willa turned to see her mom's face. Were adults used to getting surprise packages?

Grandma Edna slid out of the truck and held out her freckled arms. The present was wrapped in brown paper, tied with twine.

"Hi, Mom." The kids' mom tucked the seed packet in the pocket of her gardening apron.

"Hello, dear," Grandma responded. "This is something to help you on your way."

Willa and Ben exchanged glances. Grandma Edna almost always said what was on her mind. But lately they had noticed that she was dropping hints. She didn't always say what she really meant. Willa wondered if she was doing that now.

Mom started to pull at the wrapping, but then Ben rushed forward and ripped the paper wide open. "What is it?" Ben asked.

"It's a banner," Grandma said. "It says 'Grand Opening.' It is for your bed-and-breakfast. You'll have a full house next weekend."

Mom gasped. "What?"

"My friend runs an inn on the far side of the island," Grandma explained. "She accidentally double-booked all her rooms, so I said you would take her extra guests."

"What?" Mom repeated.

"You really can't put off opening this inn any

longer, dear," Grandma Edna said. "You and Eric have to be in business by summer if you want to be a success."

"Did I hear Edna Miller out here?" Dad appeared on the porch, holding a whisk in his hand. He was smiling.

"My mom just found us a house full of guests for next weekend," Mom told Dad.

"An inn full of guests," Grandma Edna corrected. "You are about to officially open your bed-and-breakfast. It isn't just a house anymore. It's an inn."

Grandma returned to her truck and, before she drove away, called out the window, "I'm excited for you!"

Willa looked at Dad. The whisk now dangled at his side. His smile was gone.

Next Willa looked at Ben. He had been staring at Starbuck, but he glanced back at his sister. Willa could tell he was as worried as she was. If the two of them wanted to stay on Chincoteague and keep Starbuck, they would have to get to work.

Chapter 2

"THAT IS *VERY* SOON," DAD SAID. HE WAS LOOKING at the calendar on his phone. Dad walked over and sat down on the porch swing. "Seriously soon," he added.

"I can't believe my mother did this to us," Mom replied.

"If it's a grand opening, the restaurant has to be ready too," Dad realized out loud. He rubbed his chin. "I don't even have a produce supplier yet."

Willa knew what a produce supplier was. Dad had used one at his job back in Chicago. "Produce" was a word for fruits and vegetables. The "produce supplier" brought all the fresh food directly to the restaurant so Dad wouldn't have to go to the grocery store to shop for everything.

"And I'll have to tell Russo's I won't be able to work nights anymore." Dad had been filling in as a cook at an Italian restaurant. He wouldn't be able to work both places at once.

Ben stared at Willa. The whole reason their family had moved to Chincoteague Island was so Dad could open his own restaurant and Mom could run a bed-and-breakfast. At first,

Willa and Ben hadn't been sure it was a good idea. They had liked Chicago, and they had liked their friends there. But, after a while, Chincoteague had begun to feel like home. They had made wonderful new friends. Most of all, they now had Starbuck. If their parents' plans for Misty Inn didn't work out, it would mean another move for the Dunlaps. The kids understood that. They also knew that a different town would mean a lot more changes. Chances were that they wouldn't be able to take Starbuck with them. Neither Willa nor Ben could bear the thought of that.

Willa could feel the worry churning in her belly. She had to do something. "You're both being silly," she announced. "Grandma's right. It's time to get cracking."

Mom and Dad raised their eyebrows but didn't say a word.

Willa walked over to Mom, who was scowling at a long, narrow strip of paper that she had pulled out of her pocket. Willa gently pulled the paper from Mom's hand. It was a list. She skimmed it.

* order new mailbox
* plant rosebushes
* paint parking sign
* buy vases for dinner tables
* AND a lot of other things

"There isn't anything on here that *has* to be done before we open, is there?" Willa insisted, not waiting for either of her parents to answer.

"We don't need more to-do lists; we just need to do it."

Of course, Willa had never opened a bed-and-breakfast before. She didn't know exactly what was and wasn't needed. She just needed to convince her mom and dad that they were in good shape. She sure hoped they were, anyway.

Last fall the Dunlaps had all worked to get the bed-and-breakfast ready for its first visitors. In order to make it happen, Mom had stopped talking about all the things they had to do and had started making lists instead. Ever since the success of that trial weekend, Mom had kept making lists. She had made hundreds by now. She could always find more ways to improve Misty Inn.

It wasn't that Willa didn't like lists. She

actually *loved* lists, even more than Mom. But she knew when enough was enough.

"And, Dad," Willa added, thinking fast, "sure, you'll need a produce guy. But think about all the stuff you already have." She took Dad by the hand. She led him into the kitchen and opened the pantry door. Ben followed right behind.

The pantry at Misty Inn was no ordinary pantry. Willa had seen pictures of the closets of famous actresses and singers, with shelves for shoes and color-coded hangers for fancy gowns. She thought of her dad's pantry as the same thing, but for chefs.

"Just look," Willa said. "You are totally set."

In one glance, Willa saw seven types of salt, four different kinds of paprika, and more than a half dozen brands of flour. Vanilla extract, vanilla beans still in the pods, and vanilla syrup. There were also dried versions of all the herbs Mom had planted in the flower beds, hanging in upside-down bouquets from the top shelf. "Dad, you're a chef. You love to make food. You should be excited to get started."

Ben reached out and pulled a stack of hand-written recipes off the shelf. He handed them to Dad. "Time to cook *your* recipes, Dad."

Their dad had always worked for a big restaurant, and another chef, often a famous one, had been in charge. The restaurant at Misty Inn was not big, but it was Dad's first chance to be the head chef. It was his first chance to make his own menu with all his own recipes, too.

"You know, kids, I think you're right," Dad admitted, smiling at Willa. He held the food-stained pages of recipes in one hand and pulled Ben close with the other. "Thanks, you two. Mom and I needed the pep talk."

"Just a little tighter," Mom called to Dad. "And to the left."

It was the next day, and Dad was up on the roof of their house. It seemed like he had been there for an hour. Willa and her friend Sarah Starling had ridden bikes, played five rounds of War with cards, and staged four tree-climbing races since he had first crawled out the upstairs window.

Dad was putting up the GRAND OPENING banner. Mom wanted it to hang between the two

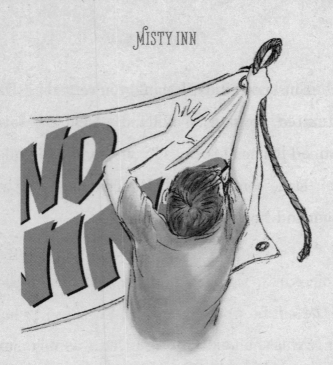

windows on the third floor. Willa kept her eye on him as she played.

Dad inched his way toward the far side of the banner. His body was tilted forward and his feet were spread wide as he tried to keep his balance. A brisk wind was coming from the ocean. It whipped the banner right out of Dad's hands.

"You need to secure the bottom corners,"

Mom instructed. Willa caught her breath as Dad stumbled forward. The wind lifted his baseball cap off his head.

"Dad, come down!" Willa yelled. She ran over to where Mom watched.

"I've almost got it," he insisted, raising his voice.

"He'll be fine," Mom said, resting her hand on Willa's shoulder. "Your dad's very sure-footed."

Just then a rumble sounded. Willa looked up and spotted a black cloud. It seemed like it had appeared out of nowhere. It now hung directly over Assateague.

Assateague was the thin barrier island that lay between Chincoteague and the open sea. It was home to two herds of wild ponies.

From up where Dad was, he could probably see the old lighthouse on Assateague. The red-and-white lighthouse had been there for more than a hundred years and still shone a beam as a warning to ships at sea.

Another roll of thunder sounded like hooves pounding across the sky. The black cloud was crossing the bay.

"Dad, hurry!" Willa cried. Sarah had now joined her next to Mom.

Mom was glancing out toward the sea. "Yes, dear. Hurry! A storm is coming."

"Sarah! Sarah!" It was Ben, running from up the street. He had been at the Starling's. "You have to go home. Your parents told me to tell you they need help getting the animals in before it rains."

"But the horses and goats can stay out in the rain," Sarah said with a shrug.

"I don't think this is just any rain, Sarah," Mom said, looking at the dark clouds spreading across the sky. "You should head home now, sweetie."

A growl of thunder forced Sarah and Willa to say their good-byes. As soon as Sarah reached the end of the driveway, plump raindrops began to fall.

Chapter 3

IT DIDN'T TAKE MOM LONG TO CHECK THE
weather forecast on her phone. When she did,
she insisted Dad get down right away.

"Don't worry about the banner," Mom called.
"We can open the inn without a banner. We can't
open without *you*!"

As soon as she saw Dad crawl back through the
window and give a thumbs-up sign—indicating

he had hung the banner in spite of the weather—Mom put the rest of the family to work.

Willa and Ben's first job was to bring Starbuck and Buttercup inside. The animals would be safer—and drier—in their stalls with flakes of hay to keep them busy. Of course, Amos also needed his dinner since he'd stay with the horses. Next the kids rolled their bikes into the barn.

The few raindrops falling were heavy and thunder kept booming. Slate-colored clouds were above, bringing on an early night.

Mom hurried around, making sure all the old house's shutters were latched closed. She turned over the outside furniture. "Search the yard for anything that could be lifted and carried by a strong wind," she said, picking up a rake and a short shovel. When she put her gardening tools in the barn, she grabbed a bungee cord.

"Help me with the grill!" Mom yelled to Willa, waving the cord over her head.

Willa hurried over to the patio, her arms wet with the rain. The wind crept into her cotton dress, making it balloon out in all directions. "You really think this thing is going anywhere?" Willa asked, looking at the big black appliance with the propane tank underneath.

"Best to be on the safe side," Mom yelled over the swirling wind. She stretched the colorful cord around the deck railing and then handed the other hooked end to Willa.

"I think it's better to be *inside*," Willa answered. She tugged on the cord until it was tightly secured around the barbecue.

"Yes," Mom agreed. "Let's go." She grabbed Willa's hand and they ran, their hair and clothes streaming behind them. They escaped inside through the kitchen door just as a clash of thunder cracked in the sky.

The rumbles of thunder and patter of rain were muffled in the big house. Willa immediately felt more at ease when Mom wrapped her in a towel. "I'm going to get dry clothes," she said with a shiver. She passed Ben on the stairs.

"It's movie weather!" Ben announced, his sleeping bag trailing behind him.

"I'll make popcorn," Dad offered. Willa saw Mom roll her eyes. Willa guessed her mom was still in high gear, wanting to do more to fix up the inn.

"Come on, Amelia," Dad said, his head in the pantry. "Mother Nature is telling us to take a break. I can make you a bowl without butter."

"Popcorn without butter?" Mom asked. "What's the point?" She smiled at Dad.

"Come help pick a movie," Ben called from the sofa. And that's when the lights flickered and went out.

"The TV died," Ben groaned. "No movie."

"What's Mother Nature telling us now?" Mom wondered out loud.

"Popcorn and board games by candle-light!" Willa said from the landing. She then rushed down the stairs and opened the game cabinet. She didn't want to miss out on family time. "That's exactly what Mother Nature's saying."

The Dunlaps played through the howling wind and pouring rain. The kids flinched when the crackles of the storm were fierce, but they huddled close. They played until Willa and Ben were too tired to climb the stairs for bed, so they slept—in sleeping bags—on the family-room floor. They knew they wouldn't be allowed to do anything like that when the inn was full of guests.

"Look at this," Mom grumbled as she opened the front door. It was the next morning, and the yard was a soggy patchwork of sticks and leaves. A thin layer of sand covered everything.

The kids checked on Starbuck and Buttercup first thing. When they opened up the barn, Starbuck whinnied a hello. Even though the pony didn't like to be cooped up, Willa knew they couldn't put her or Buttercup out in the field. The ground was still too wet.

Dad approached from the other side of the house. "I've got some bad news," he said. Willa and Ben followed their parents around to the back, the toes of their rain boots sinking in the marshy grass.

"Apparently those lightning flashes were closer than we thought." Dad pointed to a tree. It was an old black willow, its branches reaching higher than the house.

"It lost a limb," Ben whined.

"It broke a window," Dad added. He pointed toward the house. "In our *best* guest room."

"Do you think there's water damage?" Mom asked.

"There's only one way of knowing," Dad answered, looking up to the third floor. "When we moved to be by the water, I didn't plan on so much of the water actually being in our house." Last year they had had a plumbing problem that had flooded the whole top floor.

"That was just one other time," Mom insisted.

"One time, but weeks of cleanup." Dad bent down, starting to gather some of the sticks and small branches that littered the ground.

"I don't want to know what Mother Nature is telling us now," Ben grumbled.

"She's telling us to stop worrying about little things and just deal with the big stuff," Willa said in a bright, optimistic voice. Personally, Willa couldn't believe that they had to deal with another setback, but she didn't want her parents to feel discouraged.

"This is big all right," Dad agreed. "A big mess."

"I'll go and check on the room upstairs," Mom said. Her feet squished as she walked away.

"Ben and I can pick up the yard," Willa volunteered. "We are here to help!"

Dad sighed. "Thanks, but I should check for broken glass and other stuff first." He took another deep breath, checking out the damage. "But you're right, Willa. In the big scheme, things aren't that bad. How about you go look in on our neighbors? Start with Mrs. Cornett. Make sure she's okay."

"Good idea, Dad," Willa replied. "Mrs. Cornett's

chickens are wacky enough as is. I hope they weren't too scared during that storm."

"They were probably running around like chickens with their heads cut off!" Ben said, laughing so hard he could barely talk.

"Ben, that's gross," Willa scolded. "And not very funny."

"Maybe not to you," Ben said. "Or the chickens." He closed his lips tight, but giggles escaped out his nose.

"Good luck," Dad said, patting their backs, as they walked off toward their neighbor's house.

"You too!" Willa called.

Mrs. Cornett lived by herself. Her house was the next one down the road from Misty Inn. It wasn't far, but there was a cluster of trees in between so you couldn't see the little yellow cottage with lots of plants and flowers.

Willa hoped Dad's suggestion was a sign that they weren't that bad off, that they should take time to think of others. Of course, there was also the chance that Dad was just trying to get rid of them so he and Mom could sulk about the inn on their own.

Chapter 4

"I'M SO GLAD YOU KIDS CAME BY," MRS. CORNETT said. "That storm scared the eggs right out of my hens. I have more eggs than the Easter Bunny. I keep finding them all around the yard."

Mrs. Cornett must have been up for hours. She had already made several dozen of her famous deviled eggs, and she was starting to "whip up" something else. Tan, white, and pale-blue eggshells were piled by the cutting board.

"She seems fine," Willa whispered to Ben. They were in Mrs. Cornett's kitchen, which looked like a diner from an old movie, with a shiny metal counter and tall bar stools. "No trees fell on her house. Maybe we should go home and help there."

"Yeah," Ben answered. "Maybe."

"I tell you what, kiddos." Mrs. Cornett reached for a big metal bowl as she spoke. "You herd up my loose hens, and I'll make you some scrambled eggs. They'll be fluffy. I prom-ise you that."

"It's a deal," Ben said, pushing himself off a stool.

"I don't think eating a second breakfast is

what Dad had in mind when he sent us over here," Willa said under her breath, hoping Mrs. Cornett wouldn't hear. Willa wondered how Mom and Dad were doing back at the inn.

"Chasing chickens sounds like fun. And you heard Mrs. Cornett," Ben said. "She needs help. We're doing her a favor."

"You kids sure are," the woman said. "I'm too old to chase those silly birds."

Just a few minutes later Willa and Ben were outside, panting.

"Try to get Hattie," Willa said, stopping to catch her breath. "She's the ringleader."

Hattie was a striking-looking chicken. Each of her bright white feathers had a black border, and her comb and wattle were cherry red against the yellow of her sharp beak. The kids knew it was sharp. Mrs. Cornett had the scars as proof. The hens were always escaping the coop. They often wandered over to the Dunlaps' yard, and Hattie was the hardest to convince to go home.

Ben tiptoed behind Hattie as she pecked in the strawberry patch. The chicken didn't seem to notice Ben. But as soon as he spread his

arms wide for the capture, she jutted off, cluck-ing and flapping her wings. The other chickens scattered, and Ben collapsed in the grass . . . smack onto an egg!

"Yuck," Ben screeched. Raw egg dripped from his hand.

"You thought this would be fun?" Willa said, wiping sweat from her face. She leaned against the trunk of a fruit tree.

"I was wrong," Ben admitted.

As soon as the chickens were back in their coop, Mrs. Cornett asked the kids to pick bush beans and peas from her garden. It was nearly lunchtime before they were done. After their meal of scrambled eggs, she sent them off with a basket of what they had harvested, plus some ruby-red radishes.

As they walked home, Willa noticed that despite all the wind and weather, the GRAND OPENING banner had remained in place. It didn't even look battered. The letters were bold and bright.

Still, Willa had a bad feeling. The more she thought about it, the more she believed Dad had been trying to get rid of them so he and Mom could deal with the inn on their own. They could never finish without help. As she and Ben walked past the front porch on the way to the kitchen door, she could hear her parents' raised voices through the open windows.

"But why are all the flashlights in the closet on the *first* floor?" Mom asked.

"It just makes sense to store them together," Dad insisted.

"But what if the lights go out and we're all

on the *third* floor?" Mom said. "That's where the guests will be."

Willa grabbed Ben's elbow before he reached the door. "We can't just walk in. They're arguing."

"The electricity is back on," Ben whispered, confused. "Who cares where the flashlights are?"

Willa shrugged. She guessed the quarrel wasn't *really* about flashlights.

But now it seemed like things had quieted down. She looked at Ben, and he raised his eyebrows. Just as she was about to turn the doorknob, she heard a door slam. "And where are all the batteries?" Mom yelled.

"In the toy bin under Ben's bed!" Dad called back.

"Why are they there?"

Willa and Ben sat down on the steps by the door. At least they had Mrs. Cornett's sugar snap peas to snack on while they waited for the argument to end.

From where they sat, Willa and Ben could see inside the open barn doors. They could just make out Starbuck's head as she nibbled from her hay net. They would both visit her later, but they had to have an important brother-sister discussion first.

They made a pact, a solemn promise, that they would do whatever they could to help Mom and Dad. They hated when their parents argued, even when it was about a silly thing like a flashlight—*especially* when it was about a silly thing like a flashlight!

They agreed they would take on whatever

jobs they could, and they would not let their parents tell them not to help. It was their house too! They would be ready for the inn's opening. It was Sunday, and the guests were coming on Friday.

All along, the plan had been to call the bed-and-breakfast Misty Inn and the restaurant the Family Farm. Willa had always liked the name of the restaurant. It sounded so cozy and welcoming. But at that moment, crouched on that narrow step, Willa didn't think the house felt cozy *or* welcoming. They had less than a week, but Willa was going to do her best to make that name fit!

Chapter 5

MOM AND DAD NODDED AND SMILED AS THE KIDS presented their plan at dinner that night. Their parents admitted things had been hectic. "We promise to give you a list of ways you can help," Mom said. "But there are just some chores kids can't do."

"Or parents," Dad added. "Most parents can't replace a one-hundred-year-old window.

We were lucky we found a carpenter who can do it this week."

"You can have my room," Ben offered out of nowhere, his cheeks turning pink. "For the inn, if you need it. I'll clean it and everything." He hadn't even touched the sausage meatballs on his pasta. They were his favorite.

Willa watched as Mom and Dad looked at each other. She wondered what they were thinking. "That's very sweet, Ben," Mom said. "But we'll be fine. It'll all get done, and you can stay in your own room. This may soon be an inn, but it will always be your home, too." Mom's eyes were warm and kind when she looked at Ben, but her expression changed as she glanced down at her plate.

"I just remembered!" Willa yelled out. "It's a teacher prep day on Friday, so we don't have school. We can help right up to the moment the guests come!" Willa felt so relieved. She and Ben could really make a difference then.

Mom and Dad didn't look so sure. "We'll see," Dad said. "Maybe all the work will already be done."

"Maybe," Willa said, trying to sound as reassuring as possible, but she could tell her parents were worried, which made *her* worry too. After giving Dad a hand putting the dishes in the dishwasher, Willa sneaked out to the barn.

Starbuck and Buttercup were still in their stalls. Clouds had lingered in the sky all day, so the sun had not had a chance to dry the pasture. Willa first offered Buttercup a treat of carrot tops before heading over to spend time with Starbuck.

Starbuck nickered, stretching her neck for her own treat. The pony eagerly ate the green stems and rested her head over Willa's shoulder. "Sorry, no actual carrots today," Willa told Starbuck. "Dad's saving up for the restaurant recipes." Starbuck didn't seem to feel cheated. She seemed content. It comforted Willa, hearing the even munching of the pony's jaw, her easy breath.

Tomorrow was Monday. Willa had hardly thought about school, other than how no school on Friday would give her and Ben time to help. At the beginning of the school year, she and Ben had always been busy. They had wanted to try to finish their chores at home so they could hurry to Grandma Edna and Grandpa Reed's farm to see Starbuck. Once the pony had come to live at Misty Inn in the fall, they had not had to rush around all the time.

"I hope we'll have time for a ride this week," Willa murmured. Starbuck sighed. It seemed to Willa that the pony understood how important the opening of the inn would be. Willa wrapped her arms around the pony's neck. "I hope so," she said again.

♥

Willa and Ben were true to their word. They did extra chores every evening to get the inn closer to being ready. Because she had nice handwriting, Mom had Willa make a sign for the check-in table and place cards for all the guests at dinner. Just to get the hang of it, she practiced by making a card for both herself and Ben. Ben's job was to roll the fancy silverware in the cloth napkins for dinner.

"Why are we doing this little stuff when there's still a hole in a bedroom window upstairs?" Ben wondered as he lined up the napkin corners.

"Because we do what we can," Willa said, admiring the new dining-room setup. There were now five wooden tables for guests to use while enjoying breakfast or dinner. The tables didn't match, yet each had its own charm. It was starting to look like a real inn! But each day there were also little setbacks.

The carpenter had come to install the guest-bedroom window on Wednesday. The replacement looked as good as new, but the carpenter tripped on the porch steps on his way out. His foot went straight through a rotten board. "I'm all booked tomorrow," he said. "But I can come back to fix it Friday morning."

Willa and Ben passed the carpenter in the driveway as they got off the bus. After the man drove off, Dad collapsed on the front lawn. "As soon as he replaces the board, we have to paint it, and the paint has to dry before anyone can use the stairs." He paused, his baseball hat pulled over his eyes. "Even if he shows up first thing Friday, that's cutting it close."

Mom bent down to pat Dad on the shoulder, but she only comforted him for a minute. "Okay, kids," she then announced. "Out of your school clothes. You have a manure pile to move."

"Do we *really* have to move the manure?" Ben asked moments later, holding his nose with one hand and a pitchfork in the other.

"You can unplug your nose," Willa said. "It's so old it doesn't smell that bad anymore." Willa knew what he meant—the job didn't seem super important. Still, Willa was going to move every chip of manure from where they'd stacked it for months on the side of the field to the spot behind the barn, right where Mom had pointed.

Even if it wasn't an important job, it was a

big one. The wheelbarrow tipped over ... twice. Ben lost his footing and ended up sitting in the stuff. *Gross!* And even though she thought she was careful, Willa had two boots full of dry horse poop before they were done.

"Why do we have to eat out here with the bugs?" Ben groaned when the family took a dinner break.

"It keeps the crumbs outside," Mom had explained. "And the kitchen clean. Unlike you." Ben half smiled, his teeth a bright white against his now-dirty skin.

Many blisters and drinks from the hose later, the brother-and-sister shoveling team was done. "I love Starbuck," Ben said, putting the pitchfork back in the barn, "but I wish she could use a toilet."

"We should clean up in the downstairs bath-room," Willa said as they headed inside, "so we don't track all over the house."

They left their filthy boots outside and then crammed inside the little bathroom, elbows and feet barely fitting. "Use soap," Willa reminded Ben. He picked up the bar and started to make suds. They watched as the bubbly water, brown with dirt, dripped from their hands.

They were almost finished when they heard footsteps. "Willa? Ben?" The door was flung open. "What are you doing in there?" Mom looked as if she had caught them in a trash dump.

"We're washing up so we don't make a mess upstairs," Willa said, proud that she had thought ahead.

Mom looked like she was about to cry. "This

was the one bathroom that I *had* cleaned."

Willa looked around and realized that the bar of soap had been new, and the towel, now crumpled in Ben's hands, had a fancy lace border on the bottom. *Oops!*

"Grandma wants to talk to you," Mom said, and she placed her cell phone in Willa's hand.

As Willa left the bathroom, she noticed a note pasted to the outside of the door.

CLEAN! DO NOT USE!

THANKS,

MOM

Chapter 6

"I REALLY DON'T KNOW, GRANDMA," WILLA SAID.
"Ben and I wanted to stay home and help with
the opening. Can we tell you tomorrow?" Ben
tried to push in closer. "Okay, bye."

"What'd she say?" Ben asked. He'd been
standing by her shoulder, his ear tilted toward
the phone.

"She wants to know if we want to go to

Assateague on Friday," Willa answered. "She's doing a special vet check on the wild ponies."

"Friday?" Ben asked. Willa nodded. Even though it was just a boat ride away, the Dunlap kids had not visited Assateague yet. To them, the tiny island that was the remote home of the famous Chincoteague ponies was still a mystery. Ever since Starbuck had come to live with them, they both felt like they had their own piece of the Assateague legend right there in their old red barn.

"What's on Friday?" Mom asked, striding into the kitchen, her arms full of candlesticks.

"The opening of the inn," Willa replied innocently.

"No," Mom said, shaking her head. "Something to do with Grandma."

Willa reluctantly told Mom about Grandma Edna's invitation.

"Well, you have to go!" Mom said. "It's such a good opportunity."

"But we want to stay here and help you and Dad," Willa said.

"Yeah," Ben chimed in.

"I think your dad will agree with me," Mom said.

Willa suspected that Mom wanted them to go, but not just because it was a good opportunity. She glanced hopefully at the clock. "Well, it's nearly bedtime," Willa said all of a sudden, raising her hands in an exaggerated shrug. "And it's a family rule that we can't make big decisions after eight o'clock. I guess it'll have to wait for tomorrow."

Mom rolled her eyes.

Willa had always thought it was a silly rule, but she was thankful for it now.

The next morning on the school bus, Sarah begged Willa to go on the trip. "You have to," Sarah said, grasping Willa's hand. "Dad is taking me and Chipper. Kids hardly ever get to go to the roundups on the island. It'd be so much fun to be there together."

Grandma had explained the details to Willa on the phone. The volunteer fire department of Chincoteague helped take care of the ponies. Three times a year a group of volunteers and local veterinarians gathered the wild ponies for checkups. The roundup in the middle of the summer included the great pony swim, when all the horses and ponies of the southern herd swam across the bay to Chincoteague.

The spring roundup was not as complicated. While the events of the pony swim took the entire weekend, this spring roundup would be done in a day. All the ponies would stay on Assateague.

"We can take our walkie-talkies," Chipper said to Ben. The idea made Ben smile. Now that he knew Chipper would be there, he wanted to go more than ever. He glanced at Willa. He could tell she hadn't decided.

"I'm not sure," Willa tried to explain. "My parents never hired a server for the inn, and Dad might need to run some last-minute errands. They might need me."

"You need a waitress?" Chipper asked, overhearing the girls' conversation. "Katherine keeps telling Mom she needs a job. She wants to buy a car." Katherine was the oldest of the Starling kids.

"Is that true?" Willa asked Sarah.

"Well, yeah," Sarah replied. "She does."

"That's huge!" she exclaimed. "I'll bet Mom would hire her in a second." With that good news, Willa felt like things would come together. She felt like she and Ben could enjoy a trip to Assateague with Grandma and their friends. She convinced herself that Mom and Dad could take care of the last-minute details by themselves. They were grown-ups, after all.

"Katherine? That's great," Mom said. "I'll call the Starlings right away."

Willa had finally found Mom in Ben's bedroom, ironing pillowcases.

"So, Ben and I decided to go to Assateague with Grandma tomorrow," Willa announced.

"Oh?" Mom replied. It was not the reaction Willa expected.

"Sarah and Chipper will be there," Willa explained. "And I double-checked with Grandma that we'll be back by evening. I can even probably help with dishes."

"Well, I don't think you'll need to do that," Mom said with a slight smile. She set the iron down and took a sheet of paper from her pocket. A list. She made a tiny clucking sound as she reviewed it. "Sweetheart," she began again, looking up at Willa. "I know you've been busy, but there are Popsicle sticks in the craft bin. Would you make markers for all the herbs?"

Willa couldn't tell if Mom was giving her silly

little jobs just to keep her busy. "But, Mom, I want to really help."

"That will be help," Mom answered.

As she headed down the stairs, Willa passed Dad on his way up. "Your brother needs a brush so he can make a 'Wet Paint' sign for tomorrow," Dad said. "Can you get him one? He's in the barn."

"Of course," Willa said.

"And keep an eye on the corn bread in the oven?" he called out from the second floor.

"Yes," Willa replied, making a list in her head.

First she located a paintbrush in the cupboard under the stairs. She ran it out to Ben, who was looking for leftover wood for the sign. When she came back to the house, she headed straight for the craft bin so she could make the markers for the garden. Then the doorbell rang. It was Katherine Starling, already there to ask about the job.

Willa called to Mom and heard a scratching at the back door. "New Cat? How did you get out?" Willa wondered as the cat strutted into the kitchen.

That's when Dad raced down the stairs. "Did you take out the corn bread?" he asked.

"Not yet," Willa said, looking at the clock. "The buzzer didn't go off."

"I didn't set one," Dad said. "I told you to keep an eye on it."

Willa had been busy doing other things! Didn't he get that?

Dad pulled the corn bread out. She could

see that the edges were tinged brown, darker and drier than Dad liked. It wouldn't be good enough for opening day.

"Don't worry, honey," Dad said. "I can make another batch tomorrow. It's always tastier fresh from the oven anyway." Dad placed the pan on the counter and pulled off the oven mitt. "Oh, I almost forgot, can you go find your mother? She wants you to show Katherine where we store some of the stuff around here."

All of a sudden, things felt very busy. Willa wondered whether she should stay home the next day. But the more she thought about it, the more she didn't want to. . . .

Chapter 7

"RISE AND SHINE. IT'S A BIG DAY."

Mom gave Willa's shoulder a shake before opening her bedroom curtains.

"It's a big day for you, too," Willa replied, squinting as light filled her room.

"You've got that right," Mom said. "Can you wake your brother?" Mom asked. "Grandma needs you two ready soon."

Willa's feet dragged as she made her way to Ben's room.

"Wake up, you," she said, throwing a stuffed hippo at Ben's head. "We're going to Assateague, and Mom and Dad are going to open an inn."

Ben sat straight up. "So I'm not battling a nest of dragons in the underworld?" he mumbled.

"Definitely not," replied Willa. "You need to stop playing video games right before bed."

"That's the only time I'm allowed to play them." Ben sulked.

"Get dressed," Willa said. "And close your door. You don't want any guests seeing this mess. Why aren't those clothes in the laundry bin?"

"Because they aren't dirty," Ben answered.

"You wore them to move the manure pile. Remember?" Willa told him, and stomped out of the room.

Even though they didn't agree on how dirty his clothes might be, Willa and Ben did agree that they needed to be home to assist Mom and Dad that night. As Willa was grabbing granola bars for their breakfast, she noticed a stack of long, thin papers next to the sink. *More lists*, she thought.

Willa was still thinking about all those lists nearly a half hour later as they climbed out of Grandma's car. Grandma led them down a sandy path where the trees arched overhead. The path ended in a hidden cove with one dock. At the dock was one small boat. They all climbed in.

"You ready?" Grandma called out as the

engine sputtered. Willa and Ben nodded and smiled, and Grandma guided the boat away from the dock using the handle on the motor.

Soon they had left the cove and entered the open water. Willa thought it was funny how normally this trip would have filled her every thought. She was crossing the bay, about to see the wild ponies of Assateague up close. Many visitors came to Chincoteague and only caught glimpses of the ponies as they escaped from the beach into the shadows of the trees. Willa knew how lucky she and Ben were.

She also thought of their Chincoteague pony back at Misty Inn. Before she had left that morning, with a chill still in the air, Willa had made sure to do her barn chores. She had thrown flakes of hay to Starbuck and Buttercup. She had made sure the large metal trough was full of water. The ponies on Assateague didn't have someone looking out for them every day. It was up to the herd to find grass for grazing and fresh water to drink.

As they sped across the bay in the cool gray of the cloudy morning, it seemed like most of the world was still asleep, except for an egret soaring in the sky. Things were very different once they arrived on Assateague.

As soon as they tied the boat to a dock, Willa could hear the whinnies.

"The cowboys should be just about done with the roundup by now," Grandma said. She lifted her vet kit from the floor of the boat. "They began near dawn, so they'll be good and ready for us."

Grandma was referring to the volunteers who helped with the roundups. The full term was "saltwater cowboys," because the cowboys and their horses often had to get in the water during the summer roundups. Sometimes, when the herd swam across the bay, there would be stragglers. It was up to the cowboys to keep the herd together.

Looking across the bay, Willa thought that Chincoteague looked far away.

"It's a shame you two haven't been to Assateague yet," Grandma said as they hiked through the sand. "I'm glad you came with me. Your folks are worried that you've been working too hard, doing too much work on the inn. I have to agree."

Willa and Ben looked at each other. Grandma

had a hard time keeping her opinions to herself. But this opinion surprised Willa. Grandma always said that kids should pull their own weight. Willa still worried that she hadn't done enough.

"Hey, look what I found!" Ben said, sifting through a clump of sea grass. "A coin! And it's old." Grandma and Willa leaned over and inspected the discovery.

Ben rubbed his finger over the silver-colored coin, brushing dirt and sand from its face. "Maybe it's from the Spanish shipwreck," Willa said. "The same one that brought the ponies to Assateague Island." Willa knew that Assateague wasn't where the cargo ship had been headed. A horrible storm had sunk the ship, but the ponies had managed to escape and swim to shore.

"See what wonders the world has to offer," Grandma murmured, on her way again. "Legend has it that you can make a wish on a coin collected from a shipwreck."

"A wish?" Ben repeated. It wasn't like Grandma to believe such things.

"A wish," she confirmed.

"Arrived on island," Ben stated in a short clip. "Found ancient coin."

Willa looked over her shoulder and realized Ben was speaking into his walkie-talkie. There was static followed by a jumble of words. Willa guessed that was Chipper responding.

"There's one of the paddocks," Grandma said, motioning ahead.

When she looked up, Willa could see Sarah with a small group by a tall white fence.

Sarah rushed forward, half running and half skipping. "Willa! You have to see this!" Sarah pulled her so close that Willa nearly bumped into her friend's extra-long, extra-high pony-tail as she ran behind her. They came to an abrupt stop at the paddock fence. "Isn't that foal the cutest!"

Sarah was right. With its deep brown eyes and wispy mane, its knobby white knees and sloppy splashes of chocolate brown on its neck and back, the foal was the cutest. It also looked like the loneliest. "Where's its mother?" Willa asked.

"The cowboys are trying to find her," Sarah answered. "She's not in this paddock or else she'd be with the foal, right?"

"Sure," Willa said, nodding. She put her elbows on the top rail of the fence and searched the paddock. It made sense that the mother would be with such a young foal. So if the mare wasn't in the fenced-in area, where could she be?

Chapter 8

"WHAT DO YOU THINK, EDNA?"

Mr. Starling and Grandma Edna were talking. All the kids were listening in. They were worried about the tiny foal, standing alone. Grandma had gone into the paddock to take a look. Now Mr. Starling wanted to hear Grandma Edna's opinion.

"I don't think they've been separated long,"

Grandma said. "The foal seems healthy and not too hungry, but he won't stay that way. He'll need milk soon."

Willa looked at the sweet foal. His eyelids drooped and then sprang open as he fought sleep.

"Someone's got to locate that mare," Mr. Starling said. "And fast." He looked at his son and daughter. He then turned to Ben and Willa. "Don't suppose you kids could help?"

"Yes, Daddy, please," Sarah begged.

"We can do it," Chipper agreed, and he handed his walkie-talkie to his dad. "Just call Ben if you need us."

Ben touched his own walkie-talkie, which was hanging from his belt. Willa realized that her brother had been quiet since the discovery of the little colt.

"I'm happy to give you all a job and get you away from the yard," Mr. Starling said, "but you can't go on your own. It's not safe."

With two other vets at the roundup, Grandma volunteered to go with them on the search for the mare.

"What'll happen if we can't find her?" Ben wondered out loud as the group marched off toward the trees.

"Well"—Grandma hesitated—"that little guy is young and still needs his mom's milk. He'll get thirsty and weak without it." Grandma walked at the lead, the kids jogging to match her pace. "But let's hope it doesn't get to that."

They first took a couple of loops around the area where the horses were corralled. Grandma thought the mare might be nearby. When they didn't see her, they headed deeper into the woods. Grandma planned to go back to where the cowboys had first spotted the herd that morning.

The island was a big place. The beach stretched for miles. There were docks and roads for tourists. Willa knew that the north side even had campgrounds, but there was also a lot of natural space. Tall pine trees shaded and sheltered the herds from the weather.

"How are we going to find a single pony?" Sarah asked after they had been hiking around for more than an hour. "She could be anywhere, especially if she darted off when the cowboys came through." Sarah said what the entire group was thinking.

"I don't know," Grandma admitted, "but the bugs have already found me."

The bugs had found everyone, and everyone was waving and swatting their hands. It made it hard to stay focused.

"What about the lighthouse?" Willa suggested. "Maybe we'll get a better view from there."

"Top-notch thinking," Grandma said. "Anyone have a compass?"

"I do," Chipper said. No wonder Chipper and her brother had quickly become such good friends. They both loved gadgets. Grandma checked Chipper's compass, changed direction, and kept swatting bugs.

They all stepped from the trees into the full light of the midday sun. They had snacked on their hike, and now they all stopped to drink water.

"It's just over there," Willa yelled, pointing to the tall red-and-white-striped brick tower. In front was a small building that looked like a one-room schoolhouse. Willa took off. Sarah ran close behind her, and the boys followed. Grandma continued at her well-paced walk.

When the girls arrived, they bolted up the two short steps to the house. Willa fumbled at the doorknob and found it was locked.

"No!" she moaned, pulling at the door.

"I thought it was *always* open," said Sarah.

Ben kicked at the sandy path.

"Did you try knocking?" Grandma asked.

At once, all four kids knocked. They were still knocking when the door swung open.

"Yes?" It was a park ranger, wearing a dark-brown hat, a tan shirt with badges, and sturdy boots.

"Please, sir, you have to let us in. We have to find a pony," Willa said.

"I don't think there are any ponies in here," the ranger replied, smiling to himself.

"No," Ben continued. "We need to use the lighthouse as a lookout. The pony is lost somewhere on the island, and her foal needs her."

The ranger's expression quickly changed. "I see," he said. "We're usually not open right now, but it sounds like an emergency." He stepped aside and motioned to the stairs.

It was a spiral staircase.

"You guys know it's haunted, right?" Chipper said, staring up.

"That's not true," Sarah said. "Even if it were, we have no choice."

"I'll wait for you here," Grandma said.

With that, Willa started climbing. The red metal steps seemed to go on forever. When she looked down, she felt dizzy. The clanging of four sets of feet rang in her ears. But she kept going. This was their best chance to find the mare. She thought of the hot sun and how thirsty the foal must be by now.

It was 175 feet straight up, and luckily the door to the metal deck was open.

"Be careful," Willa warned, holding Ben back from the railing.

The four friends looked out at the island. In places it was wooded; in others, pure sandy beach; and still others were filled with large patches of marsh grass, sprouting from the water like giant lily pads.

Willa noticed Ben take the coin out of his pocket. She realized he hadn't even shared it with Chipper. Her brother rubbed his fingers over the carved face. She wondered if he was making a wish.

"I think I can see your house!" Sarah announced. She had binoculars that the ranger had loaned to her.

"Really?" Willa asked.

"Yeah," responded Sarah. "I can see the 'Grand Opening' banner."

Willa had not thought about the inn for hours. Now she pictured her parents rushing around, Mom tending to last-minute details, Dad probably chopping vegetables.

"Where would she be?" Chipper asked under his breath.

Willa tried to answer Chipper's question. But it only made her think of questions of her own. Why would the mare not be with her foal? What could have happened? Was she okay?

Chapter 9

"WE FOUND HER! WE FOUND HER!"

Then came a frantic race down the winding staircase.

"It was Ben!" Sarah said when she reached the bottom. "Ben saw her first," Sarah explained to Grandma.

"She's not moving!" Chipper said, leaping down from the third step.

Willa and Ben were right behind the Starling kids.

Grandma quickly thanked the ranger. As they left, the kids tried to give her all the facts: The mare was not far, she seemed to be awake, and she was up to her knees in some mucky water.

"Mucky water?" Grandma said, thinking it through. "Sounds like she might be stuck. The wet sand can get slippery around here."

"Like quicksand?" Ben asked.

"Yes, in some ways," Grandma said.

Willa gulped. Quicksand did not sound good.

"Now, when we get there, I need you all to stay calm," Grandma advised. "She might very well be frightened, and you need to help her feel safe. So you stay safe too."

♥

"She doesn't seem scared at all," Sarah observed.

The mare did not seem alarmed. Her breath was steady. Her head hung low. She didn't even try to move away when the group approached. She stood still as the salt water rippled around her legs.

"Stay where the grass is thick," Grandma softly said, handing Willa a halter. "So you know you have solid ground. Nice and easy."

The pony barely blinked an eye as Willa latched the halter behind her ears. Her coloring nearly matched that of her foal.

Next Willa, still on a patch of sturdy marsh grass, attached a lead and clicked with her tongue. She tugged on the lead.

"That's right," Grandma encouraged. "Try to get her to get out of it."

The pony stretched out her neck, but she wouldn't take a step. Willa tugged harder. "Come on," she pleaded. The mare laid back her ears and strained against the halter.

"I don't think this pony is wild," Chipper said. "I think she's lazy."

"I wouldn't say that," Grandma replied.

"She's probably worn out," Ben stated. "I'll bet she tried to get loose before, and she's tired now."

"That's a good guess. So she needs a reason to move," Grandma declared. "The tide will come in soon."

Willa knew what that meant.

The water would get deeper, and it would be even harder to get the mare out!

It was nearly an hour later, and the girls had come up with a plan.

"It has to work," Willa said as she watched Mr. Starling approach. "It just has to."

In his outstretched arms, Mr. Starling carried the foal. It was slow going, as the pony was heavy. He sloshed through ankle-deep pools, headed straight for the group.

The mare had not tried to move since they had first arrived. The water had risen over her knees. While they had waited, they had poured fresh water into their hands so she could drink. Even though she was surrounded by it, the sea-water was too salty to quench her thirst.

She seemed even more tired than before, but her ears pricked forward when the stranger came close with her foal in his arms. She lifted her head and nickered a friendly greeting.

The foal returned the call, his nostrils flaring.

Willa clicked her tongue once again, hoping the paint pony would try to get herself unstuck.

"Right here, Dad," Sarah directed. The kids had decided where the foal would be safest. He needed to be away from the water, but he also needed to be close to his mother.

Mr. Starling lowered the foal onto its four

wobbly legs and then backed away. Sarah and Chipper joined him, next to Grandma.

Ben got down on his knees and wrapped his arm around the foal. "I know you want to be with her, but you can't go in the water," he said.

Willa stayed with the mare, loosely holding on to the lead. The pony stretched out her neck, but the foal was too far away. The foal reached out its neck as well.

"Come on, girl," Ben said.

The foal whinnied again, the pitch higher. The mare seemed content to stay where she was.

"What if we took him away?" Willa asked. She thought about how hard it would be to have something you love, and then deal with the idea of not having it. "She might try harder if she thought we were leaving with him."

"Nothing else is working," Grandma said, sounding discouraged.

"I think it's worth a shot," Mr. Starling said.

As soon as Mr. Starling lifted the young colt, it started calling out. Mr. Starling turned and took several steps away.

The foal's mother raised her head and whinnied, shrill and long. Fear flashed white in her eyes. "Come on," Willa said, putting pressure on the lead. The mare whinnied louder. Then Willa could see the pony's muscles tighten. Her hindquarters rounded as she strained. Her whole body seemed to pitch forward, and one of her back legs escaped the water with a splash.

"That's it, that's it," Willa said as one front leg surged out of the muck. "Keep coming." The next steps came easier, and soon the pony climbed onto the grassy ground next to Willa. She stumbled, pulling her way to her foal.

Mr. Starling moved quickly. As soon as the foal was back on his own feet, the weary colt walked to his mother. They touched noses, and the foal rested briefly under the shelter of his mother's neck, then ducked under her belly to drink milk.

"Well, that was lucky," Grandma said. "Wasn't it?"

"Lucky indeed," Mr. Starling agreed. His cheeks ballooned with air as he slowly exhaled.

"That should be his name," Sarah said. "Lucky."

Willa liked it. She thought it suited the sweet foal.

But she knew luck had had nothing to do with it.

Chapter 10

LUCKY AND HIS MOM WERE REUNITED. THE TINY foal flicked his fluffy tail as he trotted around the mare. Then he approached the four kids, eagerly sniffing their hands. "He's so friendly now," Chipper said.

"It's because she's here. Now he feels safe and can explore," Sarah explained to her brother.

Before long, Grandma told everyone they needed to head back to the roundup site.

"Can't we just leave them here?" Ben asked Grandma quietly. "She looks so tired. And Willa and I have to go home soon."

Willa had been thinking the same thing. The low sun was casting long shadows, which meant the afternoon was nearly over.

"It has been a long day for them, but they need to go back," Grandma said. "It's safer for them to be with the herd. And we need to make sure Lucky and his mom don't get stuck again, *especially* since they're so tired."

Willa led the mare, keeping close to Grandma and Mr. Starling, who took turns carrying the foal. Back at the paddock, Grandma and one of the other vets examined the young colt and his mother. They needed to confirm they were both okay. It had been a difficult day.

Once the checkup was over, Grandma took the halter off the mare. The wild pony immediately gave her head a good shake, her mane flopping from side to side.

"I'm satisfied. She seems good," Grandma said, closing the gate. She then turned to the kids, who had been anxiously waiting. "You all should be proud of yourselves. You did fine work."

Only now did the Starlings and Dunlaps realize they were shivering. The late-day sun had not dried their clothes. Their shoes were like sponges, but they had not noticed until now.

In the boat on the way home, Willa felt the worry of the day. Even with the sea air streaming past her face, her head and shoulders were still heavy.

Willa and Ben shared a silent glance. She knew they were both thinking of their parents and the inn. They had wanted to be home by now. They had wanted to be there before the guests arrived. But the sun was setting. The sky looked like different-colored jewels. The inn was probably already full.

"Funny," Grandma said, talking over the motor. "I was taking you two to Assateague so you could get a break from all the work. But you found an ever bigger project."

Willa just hoped Mom and Dad had not run into even bigger projects at home, too.

There were few words during the car ride home. Willa felt anxious as they neared the house.

"Thanks again," Grandma said. She stopped in front because the driveway was full of cars. "Want me to come in?"

"No," Willa answered quickly, already stepping from the truck. "We'll be fine. Thanks."

"Yeah," Ben said. "Thanks, Grandma."

"You're welcome," she said. "The place looks great."

Willa stood looking at the inn from the street. All three floors were glowing. A warm golden light shone from the windows. It looked pretty and peaceful from the outside, but Willa wondered what it was like inside.

Willa put a hand on Ben's shoulder, and they started walking up the driveway. They heard a door slam and were surprised to see Mrs. Cornett hurrying out the kitchen door.

"Well, hello, kiddos," she said, tucking a straw basket under her arm. "Just making a drop off for tomorrow morning. Congratulations on the inn."

"Thanks," Willa murmured, and she quickened her pace. When they passed the front porch, they saw Ben's handmade sign strung across the just-fixed front steps. WET PAINT.

Willa squeezed Ben's shoulder.

As they neared the kitchen door, Willa saw something move in the shadows.

"Hi, guys!" It was Katherine Starling, Sarah and Chipper's sister, who was helping in the kitchen. "Welcome back. Your dad just sent me out to cut some herbs."

"Do you need help?" Willa asked.

"Nope, I'm all set," she said. "They were all marked and everything."

Willa blushed, realizing she had marked the herbs. Ben stepped up and opened the door. Willa gave him a hopeful smile as they followed Katherine inside.

"Willa! Ben! I'll be right back," Mom called as she rushed into the dining area, a full plate in each hand.

"Mom looks nice," Ben whispered to Willa. Willa thought that Mom looked like Mom, but without the paint-splotched sweatshirt and wad of marked-up lists stuffed in her pocket.

"Hi, kids," Dad said, hugging them both from behind with his oven mitts on. "Are you hungry?" Dad's face was smudged, but his smile was bright.

"We saw Mrs. Cornett," Willa said, still confused by all the activity. "What was she doing here?"

"Oh! She's my produce supplier," Dad exclaimed. "At least for now. After you brought back her eggs and radishes and peas, I called her. She used to run a farm, and she has more veggies than she can eat."

"Isn't that great?" Mom had returned and chimed into the conversation. "And Katherine's amazing. Thanks for thinking of her, you guys."

"Sure thing," Ben said, snatching a cube of bread from a baking sheet on the counter. "Yum," he said, and grabbed another.

"Corn-bread croutons," Dad said. "I made them from that batch that overcooked yesterday. It was a good idea, if I do say so myself."

Willa took a bite. Buttery and crunchy. Pretty good for a burnt batch!

"You two must be starved." Mom tucked

a strand of hair behind Willa's ear. "Where do you want to eat? Here, in the kitchen. Or in the main dining room, so you can see Misty Inn all up and running?"

Willa looked toward the hallway that led to the dining room. It was lit with the same warm glow she had seen from outside. "I don't know, Mom. We're pretty dirty," she said, looking at her damp shoes.

"Don't be silly," Mom answered, wrapping Willa in a one-armed hug. "We are a family-run inn, and our restaurant is the Family Farm. I think it's okay that you're a little dirty." She lifted two plates from a stack and two sets of silverware, rolled up in a napkin. "Wash your hands and meet me at the table."

"I'll send you the best dish, for my two

best customers." Dad waved at them with his spatula and turned back to the stove top, which was full—full of pans that were sizzling, boiling, and simmering with good smells.

Willa and Ben sat down at a small table by a window. There was a view of the field. The night was clear and warm, and Starbuck and Buttercup were out. They looked at home.

"I hope Lucky and his mom are okay," Ben said. He placed something on the table. It was the old coin that he had found on Assateague. It was still crusted with sand in places, but the shiny parts glinted in the candlelight. Willa wanted to ask Ben if he had made a wish, but she told herself it didn't really matter.

"I hope so too," Willa agreed.

The dining room was full. The other four

tables all had guests. Everyone was talking and eating and smiling.

"Look, place cards," Ben said, pointing. "With our names."

Willa hardly even remembered making the practice cards with their names; Mom must have found them. Willa looked around. The room really did look amazing. She had been so busy, she hadn't realized just how much they had all done. But now she could see the signs of all their hard work.

Katherine brought out salads with ripe strawberries, snap peas, and corn-bread croutons. Then she came back, this time with fresh-squeezed lemonade.

"Wow, this place is nice," Ben said.

"Yeah, it is," Willa agreed. It felt cozy. It felt

welcoming. As she lifted her glass, she noticed Mom and Dad standing in the doorway to the kitchen. They had lemonade too. "Turn around," she told Ben.

Ben did, and then the Dunlaps all raised their glasses and took a sip.

The lemonade was just how Willa liked it, not too sour or too sweet.

"Here's to Misty Inn," Ben said.

"And to our home," Willa added, and they both took another sip.

ABOUT THE SERIES

Marguerite Henry's Misty Inn series is inspired by the award-winning books by Marguerite Henry, the beloved author of such classic horse stories as *King of the Wind*; *Misty of Chincoteague*; *Justin Morgan Had a Horse*; *Stormy, Misty's Foal*; *Misty's Twilight*, and *Album of Horses*, among many other titles.

Learn more about the world of Marguerite Henry at www.MistyofChincoteague.com.